Emily's Snowball
The World's Biggest

by **Elizabeth Keown**
illustrated by **Irene Trivas**

Atheneum 1992 New York

Maxwell Macmillan Canada · *Toronto*
Maxwell Macmillan International
New York · Oxford · Singapore · Sydney

To my grandchildren,
Emily, Artie, and Rebecca
—E.K.

For Emilie and Becca
—I.T.

Atheneum, Macmillan Publishing Company, 866 Third Avenue, New York, NY 10022.
Maxwell Macmillan Canada, Inc. , 1200 Eglinton Avenue East, Suite 200, Don Mills, Ontario
M3C 3N1.
Macmillan Publishing Company is part of the
Maxwell Communication Group of Companies.
First edition. 1 2 3 4 5 6 7 8 9 10
Printed in Hong Kong

Library of Congress Cataloging-in-Publication Data

Keown, Elizabeth.
Emily's snowball: the world's biggest / by Elizabeth Keown.—1st ed.
p.   cm.
Summary: With the help of friends and neighbors, Emily makes a snowball as big as a
mountain.
ISBN 0–689–31518–X
[1. Snow—Fiction.] I. Title.
PZ7.K4365Em   1992
[E]—dc20
90-1181

When Emily looked out the window, big flakes of snow were falling, and they had started to cover the ground. "I want to make a snowball," she said.

Soon Emily was outside in her backyard. She took some snow in her hands and patted it together. She rolled it on the ground, and she made a snowball. Since Emily was a little girl, she made a little snowball. But she was proud of it!

When it was time to come inside, she wanted to
bring the snowball in the house and play with it, but
her mother had her leave it on the back porch near
the door.

By the next morning, there was so much snow that all schools were closed. Emily and her older brother and sister hurried out to play. They found the little snowball, just as Emily had left it.

Emily took the little snowball with her.

"Let's make it bigger," suggested her sister, and helped the other children pack big handfuls of snow around it.

Then the children started pushing and rolling it.
Over and over the snowball rolled,
Picking up more and more snow,
And growing bigger and BIGGER!

The snowball became too big and too heavy for
Emily and her brother and sister to roll, and the other
boys and girls from the neighborhood helped them.
When they finished, Emily's snowball was big! It was as
big as all of the children put together!

That night more snow fell.

The next day everyone had to stay home. Emily and
her father went outside to see the snowball, and some of
the men in the neighborhood came over.

"Whose snowball is this?" asked one of the men.
"It's mine," said Emily.
"It's a big one!" he said. "But why don't we make it bigger?"
Soon Emily and her father and the neighbors were
working on the snowball, pushing and rolling it.

Over and over the snowball rolled,
Picking up more and more snow,
And growing bigger and BIGGER!

They pushed the snowball from one yard to another—down the street to the end of the block.
"This snowball is as big and as heavy as a tow truck!" said Emily's father.

It was too big for anyone's yard, so Emily and her
father and the neighbors rolled it across the street to the
park and left it on top of a high hill.

But the snowball didn't stay there! It kept on going! It started down the hill!

Over and over the snowball rolled,
Faster and faster!
Picking up more and more snow,
And growing bigger and BIGGER!

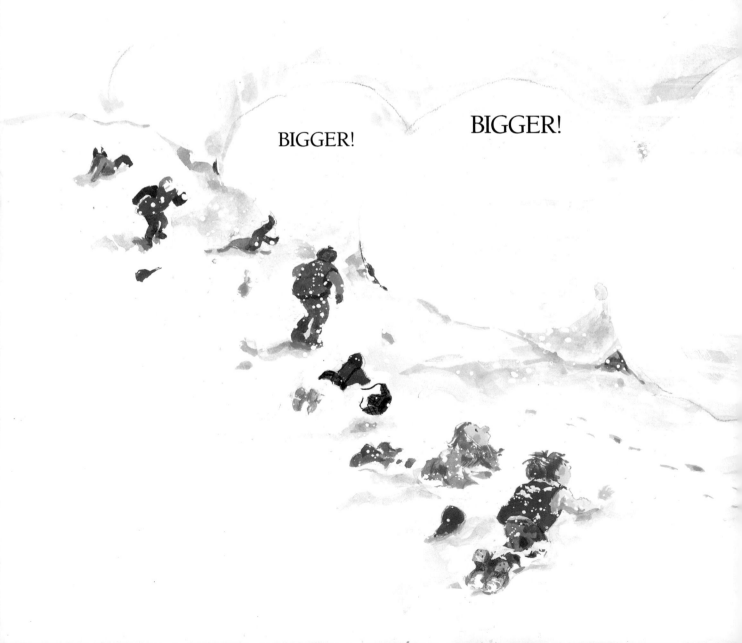

BIGGER!

BIGGER!

BIGGER!

BIGGER!

Finally, at the bottom of the hill it stopped rolling.
Emily's snowball was enormous! It was as big as an
elephant!

By the next day, the snow had stopped falling. Emily
and her mother went to the park. A big truck was
clearing the road, but it had stopped, because right in
front of it—in the middle of the road—was Emily's
snowball!

The driver got out to take a look. "I wonder whose snowball this could be," he remarked.

"It's mine," said Emily.

"You sure have a big one, little girl," the man said, "and it has to move. It's blocking everything!"

The driver got back in his truck. "Climb in," he said
to Emily and her mother, "and we'll get this snowball
out of the way."

Emily and her mother got into the truck, and the
driver started it again. Then with the help of the other
men who were working in the park, carefully—very
carefully—he pushed the snowball out of the road and
rolled it down a long, low hill.

Over and over the snowball rolled,
Picking up more and more snow,
And growing bigger and BIGGER!

The driver left the snowball near the children's playground. Then he looked at it again. "This snowball," he said, "is huge! It is as big as a mountain!"

People from everywhere came to see the snowball.
They all said it was as big as a mountain. Everybody
said it was the biggest snowball they had ever seen, and
everyone thought it had to be the world's biggest!

Teachers and scientists from the university came to
study the snowball and to measure it. They found that it
really was the world's biggest, and they put up a sign:

Emily's Snowball

WORLD'S the BIGGEST

There were stories about the snowball in newspapers
and in books, and there were pictures of Emily and her
snowball on television.

Emily's Snowball
the WORLD'S BIGGEST

All winter long the snowball stayed in the park—big as a mountain. Children wanted to climb it, so the city put a rope ladder on the snowball—up one side and down the other. Then a platform with a railing was placed on the top, and the children could stand there and look all around!

Hot Chocolate

TO THE TOP

Emily and her brother and sister came to the park
every day to see the snowball and to climb it.
Everyone loved it!

Finally the weather started to get warm. Snow melted from the ground, but Emily's snowball stayed as big as a mountain.

The sun grew warmer. Birds began to sing in the park. Slowly, the snowball started melting and turning to water.

Emily's snowball was no longer as big as a mountain.
Flowers began to bloom. Schoolchildren played
baseball in the park. Emily played in the sandbox.
The weather became warmer and warmer, and the
snowball melted more and more, and Emily's snowball

got littler and

littler and

littler and

littler.

It wasn't as big as a mountain or an elephant or a tow truck or any of the children.

It wasn't even as big as a little ball. One day when Emily went to the park, all that was left of her snowball was a puddle of water.

Emily put one foot and then the other in the puddle and splashed the water from her snowball into the bright sunshine! She splashed again and again and again until all the water was gone.

But the sign was still there, and everyone remembered:

Emily's Snowball the WORLD'S BIGGEST